PEGASUS ENCYCLOPEDIA LIBRARY

Transport
WATER TRANSPORT

Edited by: Pallabi B. Tomar
Managing editor: Tapasi De
Designed by: Vijesh Chahal, Anil Kumar and Rohit Kumar
Illustrated by: Suman S. Roy, Tanoy Choudhury
Colouring done by: Vinay Kumar, Sonu, Kiran Kumari & Pradeep Kumar

CONTENTS

Introduction 3

History of water transport... 4

Types of ships 6

Important water transport routes 12

Seaport 13

Advantages of water transport 15

Disadvantages 18

Importance to economy 19

World's famous ships 20

Test Your Memory 31

Index 32

Introduction

Like road transport, water transport has been around for thousands of years. The first kinds of water transport were probably some types of canoes cut out from tree trunks.

Early sea transportation was accomplished with ships that were either rowed or used the wind for propulsion and sometimes a combination of the two.

Ship transport was frequently used as a mechanism for conducting warfare. Military use of the seas and waterways is covered in greater detail under the navy.

Water transport has dominated in transport services for centuries until the emergence of air transport. Nowadays, ships have been designed to be much faster and to be more competitive. Although relatively slow, modern water or sea transport are significantly less costly to use compared to air transport for carrying a large number of passengers for short inter-island trips and quantities of non-perishable goods in transcontinental routes.

Ships and boats are very old inventions. Archaeologists think that people first made journeys in small boats 50,000 years ago.

3

WATER TRANSPORT

History of water transport

As man overcame the boundaries of land travel, his curiosity about the world around him increased. To his aid, man had developed a means of travelling on water even before he had domesticated the horse. The origin of the **dugout boat** is one of history's great mysteries. Historians are unable to pinpoint when or where the very first water vessel was set afloat. But the addition of the boat changed the face of transportation. Boats allowed man to, for the first time ever, cross bodies of water without getting wet!

Over time, the simple boat started including a large square piece of cloth which was mounted on a central pole. This cloth, called a sail, would turn the boat into a sail-propelled ship. This new addition gave man the ability to use waterways as a means of swift travel from one place to another, and even to travel against the current of rivers. However, the evolution of water travel didn't stop with the sail. Ships would eventually take on a sleekness as they increased in size. Before long, they would add oars and rudders and then deck covers. By Greek and Roman times, ships had grown clunky shipboard towers as well, which developed over time into the medieval stern and forecastles. By the late medieval era, these castles were built solid, as a part of the ship's basic structure. Then, by the Renaissance and the Age of Exploration which followed, ships had gained tiers of rigging and sails, becoming sleek and speedy.

Then, in the 1800s, ships began to shed their sails on the rivers once again. The advent of automation was changing transportation forever. The very first automation in ships was the cumbersome paddlewheel.

Archaeologists don't really know when sailing boats were invented. However, the Ancient Egyptians sailed boats made out of the reeds growing along the River Nile over 5,000 years ago.

History of water transport

Due to their bulky form and inability to turn easily, paddlewheel boats were confined to river travel, where they would experience calmer currents and need less manoeuvrability.

After the paddlewheel came the steamship. These vessels used coal or wood burned to heat water, which in turn created the steam pressure used to work the pistons which moved the ship. The steamship was to enjoy a long and trusted run on both rivers and seas. Then, in 1912, the first diesel-powered ship, the **MS Selandia**, was launched. That diesel engine design was to become the industrial and military standard until after World War II.

Then, in 1958, the first nuclear powered ship was launched. However, nuclear power was soon discarded by industry as too expensive and risky, though it would continue to find use in the military community.

> A triangular sail called a lateen sail was invented around 300 BC.

The landmark inventions in water transportation are:

- Cornelis Drebbel invented the first submarine (1620 AD)
- First practical steamboat demonstrated by Marquis Claude (1783 AD)
- Steamboat invented (1787 AD)
- First diesel-powered ship (1912 AD)
- Hovercraft invented (1956 AD)
- First nuclear powered ship launched (1958 AD)

WATER TRANSPORT

Types of ships

Cargo Ships

A cargo ship or freighter is any sort of ship or vessel that carries cargo, goods and materials from one port to another. Thousands of cargo carriers ply the world's seas and oceans each year; they handle the bulk of international trade. Cargo ships are usually specially designed for the task, often being equipped with cranes and other mechanisms to load and unload, and come in all sizes. Today, they are almost always built of welded steel, and generally have a life expectancy of 25 to 30 years before being scrapped.

Tankers

Tankers are ships that carries a cargo of liquid in bulk; oil and its products, liquefied gases, chemicals, wine and water. Tankers are a relatively new concept dating from the later years of the 19th century. Before this, technology had simply not supported the idea of carrying bulk liquids. Liquids were usually loaded in casks.

Tanker

Tankers can range in size of capacity from several hundred tons, which include vessels for servicing small harbours and coastal settlements, to several hundred thousand tons for long-range haulage.

Oil tankers are the largest ships on the seas and have developed from the L.C.C. (large crude carrier) to the V.L.C.C. (very large crude carrier) and then to the U.L.C.C (ultra large crude carrier).

Different products require different handling and transport. Thus special types of tankers have been built, such as 'chemical tankers', 'oil tankers' and 'LNG carriers' (a tanker designed to carry 'liquefied natural gas').

Cargo Ship

Types of ships

Hovercraft

Industrial Ships

Industrial ships are those whose function is to carry out an industrial process at sea. A fishing-fleet mother ship that processes fish into fillets, canned fish or fish meal is an example. In addition, some hazardous industrial wastes are incinerated far at sea on ships fitted with the necessary incinerators and supporting equipment. In many cases, industrial ships can be recognized by the structures necessary for their function. For example, incinerator ships are readily identified by their incinerators and discharge stacks.

Hovercraft

A hovercraft is an air cushion vehicle (ACV) that flies above any surface on a cushion of air. It is powered by an engine that provides both the lift cushion and the thrust for forward or reverse movement. It is a true multi-terrain, year-round vehicle that can make the transition from land to water without touching the surface.

The hovercraft was invented by Christopher Cockerell, an English electronic engineer in the 1950s. The first full-sized hovercraft, the SRN1 was not built and ready for testing until May 28, 1959.

Depending upon the effects of terrain and weather, the average speed of a hovercraft is 56 km/h. It is faster on ice or when going downwind, slower when on dense grass or rough surfaces, or when there is a head wind.

> **The idea for the hydrofoil (a waterborne vessel that uses underwater wings to generate lift in the same way that a plane uses wings to generate lift in air) was thought of in 1881. However, the first hydrofoil was not tested until 1905.**

7

WATER TRANSPORT

Most modern ships are pushed along by a propeller. It was patented in 1836 and soon replaced paddle wheels.

Cruise Ships

A cruise ship is a passenger ship used for pleasure voyages. Transportation in such cases is not the prime purpose, as cruise ships operate mostly on routes that return passengers to their originating port.

Cruise ships are organized much like floating hotels, with a complete hospitality staff in addition to the usual ship's crew. It is not uncommon for the most luxurious ships to have more crew and staff than passengers.

The number of cruise tourists worldwide in 2005 was estimated at some 14 million. The main region for cruising was North America (70 per cent of cruises), where the Caribbean islands were the most popular destinations.

Ferries

Ferries are vessels of any size that carry passengers and (in many cases) their vehicles travel on fixed routes over short cross-water passages. Vessels vary greatly in size and in quality of accommodations. Some on longer runs offer overnight cabins and even come close to equalling the accommodation standards of cruise ships. All vessels typically load vehicles aboard one or more decks via low-level side doors or by stern or bow ramps much like those found on roll-on/roll-off cargo ships.

The typical vessel has propellers, rudders, control stations and loading ramps at both ends. It is usually wide enough to handle four vehicle lanes abreast and may accommodate up to 100 four-wheeled vehicles.

Types of ships

Specialist Ships

It is intended to encompass classifications such as icebreakers and research vessels, many of which are owned by the government. Neither type needs to be large in size, since no cargo is to be carried. However, icebreakers are usually wide in order to make a wide swath through ice, and they have high propulsive power in order to overcome the resistance of the ice layer. Icebreakers also are characterized by strongly sloping bow profiles, especially near the waterline, so that they can wedge their way up onto thick ice and crack it from the static weight placed upon it. To protect the hull against damage, the waterline of the ship must be reinforced by layers of plating and supported by heavy stiffeners.

Damage to propellers is also an icebreaking hazard. Propellers are usually given protection by a hull geometry that tends to divert ice from them, and they are often built with individually replaceable blades to minimize the cost of repairing damage. Electric transmission of power between engines and propellers is also common practice, since it allows precise control and an easy diversion of power to another propeller from one that may be jammed by chunks of broken ice.

Research vessels, also called RV or R/V, are ships specifically designed and equipped to conduct research at sea. Research vessels are often distinguished externally by cranes and winches for handling nets and small underwater vehicles. Often they are fitted with bow and stern side thrusters in order to enable them to remain in a fixed position in spite of unfavourable winds and currents. Internally, research vessels are usually characterized by laboratory and living spaces for the research personnel.

WATER TRANSPORT

Container Ships

Container ships can carry more than 13,000 containers, which are packed with all sorts of different goods and products, food, drink, chemicals and consumer items. The container concept has revolutionised sea trade. The container ship's superstructure, bridge and main engines are often placed towards the stern, leaving a large unobstructed deck space for cargo hatchways or containers. Nearly all goods can be transported in containers, which are built in standard sizes usually of 6 m and 12 m in lengths. Containers are packed ashore at factories or inland depots, carried by road or rail to a port, shipped and only opened when they reach their destination.

Barge-carrying Ships

An extension of the container ship concept is the barge-carrying ship. In this concept, the container is itself a floating vessel, usually about 18 m long by about 9 m wide, which is loaded aboard the ship in one of two ways; either it is lifted over the stern by a high-capacity shipboard gantry crane, or the ship is partially submerged so that the barges can be floated aboard via a gate in the stern.

In 1889, Morgan Roberts wrote 'The Wreck of the Titan'. It tells the story of a massive luxury liner, called the Titan, which hit an iceberg and sank. The Titanic did exactly that 14 years later and more than 1,500 of the passengers were drowned!

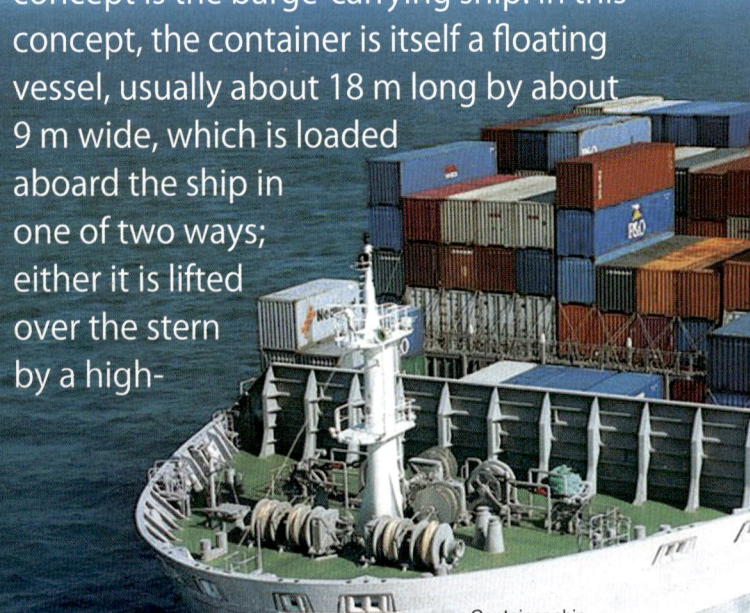

Container ship

Types of ships

Roll-on/roll-off Ships

Roll-on/roll-off ships (RORO) are specially designed ships, used to carry wheeled and tracked vehicles like cars, tractors, trucks, cranes as their major cargo load. The modern day RORO ships may even carry tanks, choppers, jets, etc. They have their own ramps or use shores ramps to load-unload the vehicles and then carry them from place to place. The cargo usually varies in height and width and hence the below deck and volume utilization is comparatively lesser than other ships and hence can be costlier as well. So they are the preferred transport for military vehicles and other such specialized jobs.

Astonishing fact

Over the years, ships and aeroplanes have vanished in the Bermuda Triangle, without trace of any wreckage. In 1880, a ship called the HMS Atalanta disappeared together with 290 crew members.

Dry Bulk Ships

Dry bulk ships transport large volume cargoes in ship loads. Major dry bulk commodities consist of industrial raw materials including iron ore, coal, grain, bauxite and alumina. Minor bulks such as soya beans/meal, steel products, phosphate rocks and sulphur also accounts for a significant part of the dry bulk trade.

Dry bulk carriers are generally designed for simplicity and cheapness. However some of the small vessels are of higher technical designs in order to trade special cargoes such as cements and rocks. These vessels are somewhat similar to multipurpose vessels in both size and design.

WATER TRANSPORT

Important water transport routes

Shipping routes reflect world trade flows. Sailings are most numerous and most frequent on routes where trade volumes are largest and demand is therefore the greatest.

Some of the important sea routes are:

> In 1935 the French warship 'Le Terrible' set a world record for speed reaching a commendable 45.25 knots (83.42 km/h) during trials.

North Atlantic Route

It is a sea route connecting Atlantic Pacific oceans through Canada. It is the busiest sea route in the world.

The Suez Canal Route

This canal connects the Mediterranean Sea with the Gulf of Suez and the Red Sea. It was opened in 1869. Earlier one had to go via the Cape of Good Hope to go to England which took almost 6 months but this canal has reduced the time taken. Now it takes only two months to reach England. It is around 160 km long.

The Panama Canal Route

The Panama Canal became operational in the year 1914. This canal connects the Atlantic Ocean with the Pacific Ocean. This canal has considerably reduced the travelling time between the two oceans. Earlier the ships had to go via Cape Horn.

There are well-established routes to the Middle East, India, Australia and New Zealand, Central and South America, as well as to East and West Africa.

In-bulk trade routes reflect the places of origin and consumption of the commodities carried. For example, many of the main oil routes begin in the Middle East and end in developed countries where demand for oil is greatest.

Seaport

A seaport is a facility which can accommodate ships which go out to sea. Seaports can be found in natural and artificial harbours along many coastlines in the world, and they have a variety of fixtures including cranes to help ships handle cargo, and docks for ships to attach to. Seaports are of economic and strategic importance to the nations which hold them, because they can be used for everything from shipping out a nation's consumer products to loading up troop ships to sail to war.

A typical seaport includes equipment and facilities for handling and storing cargo, such as warehouses and cranes, along with amenities which are designed to appeal to people coming into port, such as restaurants and hotels. Ship building and repair companies are typically located near ports for the convenience of their clients, and sea ports may also have facilities for quarantine and other special needs; a well-designed port may allow people to get everything they need without straying more than a few blocks away from their ship. Some seaports are primarily focused on cargo and commercial trade, while others cater to passenger boats like cruise ships, and many provide facilities for a mixture of uses.

Commissioned in 1797, the 'USS Constitution' won several sea battles during the American War of Independence. Amazingly she still remains on the roster of the United States Navy today as a training ship manned by a crew of 50 to 80 navy sailors.

WATER TRANSPORT

The strategic importance of a seaport can change over time. Some ports have been lost due to erosion or other issues which have caused the port to vanish or become innavigable. Others have become less important because they are no longer on major trade routes or because a nation's production of cargo has declined, making the port less profitable for shippers. The most valuable ports tend to be warm water ports, in which the water in and around the port does not freeze in the winter, allowing the port to be used year-round.

One of the most famous seaports of the world is the **National Historic Seaport of Baltimore** which is dates back to almost 300 years. Some other famous cruise ports are Boston Port-U.S.A., Norfolk Port- U.S.A., New York Port- America, Montreal Port- Canada, Philadelphia Port- U.S.A., etc.

In all there are a total of 4206 ports in the 195 countries in the world. The number of ports have increased keeping in line with the growth in sea traffic and the size of the vessels. Many of these ports serve as economy drivers for these countries and many are known for their most efficient connections across the world by means of water. The shipping industry thus forms the baseline for most part of world's export and import.

In the 1400s full rigging was developed. Full-rigged ships had two or three masts with square and triangular sails.

Advantages of water transport

Industrialized nations of the world are concerned about the environmental impacts of their activities. Studies compare the environmental impact of using rail, truck or barging for commercial transportation. Though results vary depending on the size of the barges used in the comparison, the conclusions have been the same. Barges using the inland waterways carry greater volumes for the same amount of fuel and with less environmental impact than either trucks or railcars.

It is safe

Transporting cargo safely is an important measure of environmental responsibility, and water transport has the fewest number of accidents, fatalities and injuries as compared to truck or rail.

> In the 1400s and 1500s European explorers, such as Christopher Columbus, sailed small full-rigged ships across the oceans.

Water transportation has definite advantages over competitive modes. It generally involves less urban exposure than either truck or rail, operates on a system that has few crossing junctures; and is relatively remote from population centres, all factors that reduce both the number and impact of waterway incidents.

Truck and rail tank car spills occur more often than barge spills. Barges, because of their much larger capacity, require far fewer units than either rail or truck to move an equivalent amount of cargo, and so the chance of a spill is less likely. Also, design features of barges such as double-hulls and navigational aids help reduce accident frequency.

WATER TRANSPORT

Produces little air and noise pollution

Some of the most pervasive and intrusive sources of noise and air pollution are transportation systems.

Noise levels, with road traffic the chief offender, have been rising. Air pollution comes from a wide variety of man-made and natural sources, with fossil fuel combustion the largest contributor. Air pollution caused by transportation includes pollutants directly emitted by engines as well as secondary pollutants formed by chemical reactions. Road traffic is, by far, the greatest source of air emissions.

Water transport, conversely, causes far less air pollution than trucking, and less or comparable amounts than rail. Cumulatively, it has a relatively minor effect on air quality, consumes much less energy (and as a result, produces less air pollution). For the most part, waterway operations are conducted away from population centres, which reduce the impact of its exhaust emissions. Towboats operate well away from shore, with the sound of their engines muffled below the water line, and any noise levels are hardly audible beyond the immediate area of the tow.

Causes little congestion

Other impacts of traffic congestion are accidents, increased energy consumption, environmental damage, increased commuting times and greater social tension. Water transport, in contrast, does not have congestion problems, and seldom causes them for others. The fact is that far from being congested, water transport system is under utilized.

A yacht is a vessel used for private cruising, racing or other non-commercial purposes. The lengths of yachts generally range from 8 m up to dozens of metres (hundreds of feet).

Advantages of water transport

Has minimal land use

Trains rumble through cities and trucks travel on streets and highways. Barges, on the other hand, quietly make their way along isolated waterways.

Most of the navigation way for water transport is provided by nature itself. So water transport is less likely than other transport forms to compete for land area for its navigation. Extensive land area can be taken up by new highways and railroad corridors, but apart from a few connections and waterside terminals, waterways pre-empt very little land.

A canoe is a small slender boat; about 5 m long, usually pointed at both ends, and is generally paddled by its occupants. The modern canoe is meant to hold 2-3 people, but ancient peoples built canoes large enough to carry many people and cargo.

Produces multiple benefits

Transporting bulk commodities by water has many other positive benefits and many beneficiaries.

When a new navigation project is completed, it benefits many areas including water transportation. The other major beneficiaries of developed waterway systems include recreation, flood control, public water supply, irrigation and industrial use, all uses that can be as important as the navigation project itself. Navigation not only creates opportunities for new industries, but may also change trade patterns that can have a major economic impact on local and regional development.

WATER TRANSPORT

Disadvantages

Slow Speed: Sea transport is not suitable for goods urgently needed because of its slow speed. So, not all types of goods can be transported by sea.

Documentation: Documents involved in transporting goods by sea are more in number and are very complex.

Other costs: Expenses for insurance premium, packing costs, and storage and port charges are very high and as a result increase the cost price of goods.

A row boat is a small boat that is propelled by oars. The boat can be of wooden or aluminium construction. A person sits facing the rear of the boat and pulls the oars towards his body, effectively driving the boat forward through the water.

It provides services to limited areas.

Canals maybe expensive to build and maintain.

Special maintenance for water tightness of boat is required.

It is difficult to monitor exact location of goods in transit.

Importance to economy

Increase in economic activity

If a country has a sufficient and sound infrastructure in the form of ports and waterways, the economic activity increases because many ships with tons of goods move in and out of the harbours of the country.

Increase in foreign exchange

Water transport increases foreign trade, as it increases the imports and exports of merchandise from one to the other parts of the world. International trade flourishes and trading partners are benefited a lot.

Decrease in transportation cost

Transportation cost reduces too much. Thus goods become cheap which improves the international trade between the various nations of the world.

increase in government revenue

When foreign trade increases, it not only benefits general public, but it also becomes a great source of revenue for the government by way of customs duties.

Increase in employment opportunities

Many people get jobs in the shipping industry, as in loading and unloading goods from ships. Thus directly and indirectly lots of jobs are created. This increases the general welfare of the people of the country.

A steamer or steamship, is known as such because its primary method of propulsion is steam power, which typically drives propellers. Smaller steamboats use steam power to drive paddle-wheels.

WATER TRANSPORT

World's famous ships

Supertanker-Knock Nevis

Knock Nevis was a supertanker and the longest ship ever built. Before her final journey as the MV Mont she was known as the Knock Nevis and was a Norwegian owned supertanker. Prior to that, she was known as Seawise Giant, Happy Giant and Jahre Viking. She was 458 m in length and 69 m in width, making her the largest ship in the world. She was built between 1979 and 1981 but was damaged during the Iran-Iraq War while transiting the Strait of Hormuz. She sank and was declared a total loss. Shortly after Iran-Iraq war, Norman International bought the wreckage of the ship, repaired and refloated her in 1991. After that she was used as an immobile offshore platform for the oil industry. In 2009 the vessel was sold to Amber Development Corporation, and renamed MV Mont for her final journey to Alang, Gujarat, India in December 2009 where she was beached and scrapped.

This sea giant was so large that four football (soccer) fields could be laid end to end on her deck. She surpassed the height of the Empire State Building in New York City (443 m high) and Petronas Towers in Kuala Lumpur (424 m high). She sat 24.6 m in the water when fully loaded, which made it impossible for her to navigate even through the English Channel, let alone man-made canals at Suez and Panama!

World's famous ships

Container Ship-Emma Maersk

Emma Maersk is a container ship owned by the A. P. Moller-Maersk Group. It is the world's largest container ship, longest ship currently in service and is propelled by the largest diesel engine ever manufactured. She is bigger than any aircraft carrier and manages to carry 15000 containers with only a crew of 13! She was designed for high sea travels only and unable to negotiate the Suez or Panama canals. She has a top speed of 55.8 km/h and takes about 4 days to reach Asia from US.

Emma Maersk is able to carry around 11,000 twenty-foot equivalent units (TEU) according to the Maersk company's method of calculating capacity, which is about 1,400 more containers than any other ship is capable of carrying. The vessel is 397 m long, 56 m wide, has a depth of 30 m and deadweight of 156,907 tons.

The Emma Maersk is powered by a Wärtsilä-Sulzer 14RTFLEX96-C engine, currently the world's largest single diesel unit, weighing 2,300 tons and capable of 109,000 horsepower (82 MW). The ship has several features to protect the environment. This includes recycling the exhaust, mixed with fresh air, back into the engine for reuse. This not only increases efficiency by as much as 12 per cent but also reduces engine emissions.

WATER TRANSPORT

Ocean Liner-Queen Mary 2

The Queen Mary 2 is unique. Queen Mary 2 is not only a feat in engineering, but also in size. This mighty vessel is the largest, longest and most expensive ocean liner ever built - an impressive title indeed! She is the only transatlantic ocean liner left in service. She is huge, fast, strong and has numerous unique aspects to her design that define her as an ocean liner rather than just a cruise ship.

After arriving in her home port of Southampton on Boxing Day 2003, Queen Mary 2 was named by the Queen Elizabeth II on the 8th of January before setting out on her maiden voyage to Florida on the 12th. She and her sister ship the Queen Elizabeth 2, were the only 2 true ocean liners left in the world.

On 12 January 2004, the Queen Mary 2 set sail on her maiden voyage from Southampton, England to Fort Lauderdale, Florida in the United States, carrying 2,620 passengers. On 10 January 2007, the QM2 started her first world cruise, circling the globe in 81 days.

Famous passengers or guests of the QM2 include Queen Elizabeth II, Prince Philip, Duke of Edinburgh, former French President Jacques Chirac, former British Prime Minister Tony Blair, former US president George H. W. Bush, comedian and actor John Cleese, actor Richard Dreyfuss, author and editor Harold Evans, director George Lucas, singer Carly Simon, singer Rod Stewart, CBS Evening News anchor Katie Couric and financier Donald Trump.

World's famous ships

The gondola is a world famous symbol of Venice. It is a traditional, flat-bottomed rowing boat. The main role is to carry tourists on rides at fixed prices. The gondola is moved forward by a person, the gondolier, who stands facing the bow and rows with a forward stroke followed by a backward stroke.

Bulk Carrier-Berge Stahl

The Berge Stahl is the largest bulk carrier ship in the world. An iron ore carrier, the Berge Stahl has a capacity of 364,767 metric tons of deadweight. She was built in 1986 by Hyundai Heavy Industries. The Berge Stahl is 343 m long, has a beam, or width of 65 m, and a draft, or depth in the water of 23 m.

Her Hyundai B&W 7L90MCE diesel engine is 9 m high, drives a single 9 m screw, and puts out 27,610 horsepower (20.59 MW), has a top speed of 13.5 knots, and has a 9 m high rudder.

Because of her massive size, the Berge Stahl can only tie up, fully loaded, at two ports in the world, hauling ore from the Terminal Marítimo de Ponta da Madeira in Brazil to the Europoort near Rotterdam in the Netherlands. Even at these ports, passage must be timed to coincide with high tides to prevent the ship running aground. The Berge Stahl makes this trip about ten times each year, or a round-trip about every five weeks.

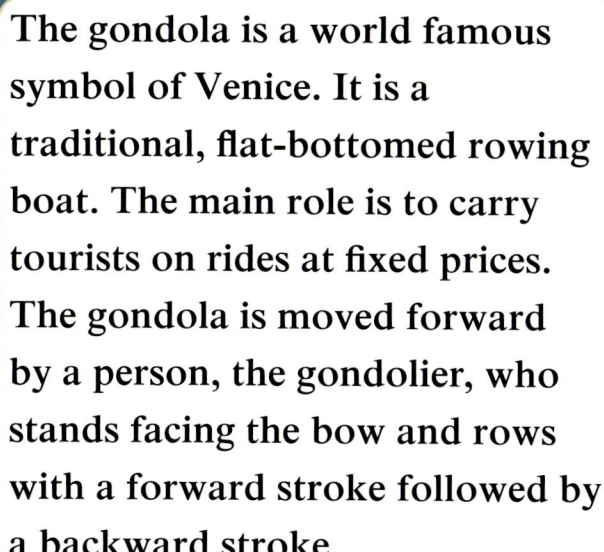

WATER TRANSPORT

Aircraft Carrier-USS Enterprise (CVN-65)

The USS Enterprise (CVN-65) is the longest naval vessel at 342 m. Due to size, she is often referred to as the 'Big E.' The Enterprise is the only aircraft carrier propelled by more than two nuclear reactors; with eight, each replaces one boiler. In addition, she is the only carrier with four rudders instead of two, and the first nuclear-powered aircraft carrier to transit the Suez Canal.

The Enterprise was commissioned in 1961 and her first air operations came in 1962 when a Vought F8 Crusader attempted a landing and catapult launch from her deck. That same year, she served the role of tracking and measuring station for Lieutenant Colonel John H. Glenn's space capsule Friendship 7. In 1964, the Enterprise, as part of the world's first nuclear-powered powerhouse (designated as Task Force One), took part in Operation Sea Orbit. It was a 65 day, 30,216 mile trip around the world, without stops for replenishment or refuelling.

The only ship of her class, Enterprise is the second-oldest vessel in commission in the United States Navy. She was originally scheduled for decommissioning in 2014 or 2015, but the National Defence Authorization Act for Fiscal Year 2010 slated the ship's retirement for 2013, when she will have served for 51 consecutive years, the most of any U.S. aircraft carrier.

> **Jet ski is a small, jet-propelled vehicle that skims across the surface of water and typically is ridden like a motorcycle. It relies on a gas-powered engine to propel themselves and a few riders through the water.**

24

World's famous ships

The gondola is a world famous symbol of Venice. It is a traditional, flat-bottomed rowing boat. The main role is to carry tourists on rides at fixed prices. The gondola is moved forward by a person, the gondolier, who stands facing the bow and rows with a forward stroke followed by a backward stroke.

Bulk Carrier-Berge Stahl

The Berge Stahl is the largest bulk carrier ship in the world. An iron ore carrier, the Berge Stahl has a capacity of 364,767 metric tons of deadweight. She was built in 1986 by Hyundai Heavy Industries. The Berge Stahl is 343 m long, has a beam, or width of 65 m, and a draft, or depth in the water of 23 m.

Her Hyundai B&W 7L90MCE diesel engine is 9 m high, drives a single 9 m screw, and puts out 27,610 horsepower (20.59 MW), has a top speed of 13.5 knots, and has a 9 m high rudder.

Because of her massive size, the Berge Stahl can only tie up, fully loaded, at two ports in the world, hauling ore from the Terminal Marítimo de Ponta da Madeira in Brazil to the Europoort near Rotterdam in the Netherlands. Even at these ports, passage must be timed to coincide with high tides to prevent the ship running aground. The Berge Stahl makes this trip about ten times each year, or a round-trip about every five weeks.

23

WATER TRANSPORT

Aircraft Carrier-USS Enterprise (CVN-65)

The USS Enterprise (CVN-65) is the longest naval vessel at 342 m. Due to size, she is often referred to as the 'Big E.' The Enterprise is the only aircraft carrier propelled by more than two nuclear reactors; with eight, each replaces one boiler. In addition, she is the only carrier with four rudders instead of two, and the first nuclear-powered aircraft carrier to transit the Suez Canal.

The Enterprise was commissioned in 1961 and her first air operations came in 1962 when a Vought F8 Crusader attempted a landing and catapult launch from her deck. That same year, she served the role of tracking and measuring station for Lieutenant Colonel John H. Glenn's space capsule Friendship 7. In 1964, the Enterprise, as part of the world's first nuclear-powered powerhouse (designated as Task Force One), took part in Operation Sea Orbit. It was a 65 day, 30,216 mile trip around the world, without stops for replenishment or refuelling.

The only ship of her class, Enterprise is the second-oldest vessel in commission in the United States Navy. She was originally scheduled for decommissioning in 2014 or 2015, but the National Defence Authorization Act for Fiscal Year 2010 slated the ship's retirement for 2013, when she will have served for 51 consecutive years, the most of any U.S. aircraft carrier.

> **Jet ski is a small, jet-propelled vehicle that skims across the surface of water and typically is ridden like a motorcycle. It relies on a gas-powered engine to propel themselves and a few riders through the water.**

World's famous ships

Allure of the Seas

The world's largest cruise ship 'Allure of the Seas,' is a new ship of Royal Caribbean International. The 'Allure of the Seas' is an architectural fantasy on the sea. It spans 360 m from bow to stern, and its height from sea level is 72 m. It weighs 600 tons – 12 times more than the Eiffel Tower.

There are altogether 16 decks and 2,704 passenger cabins in the vessel, which maximum capacity is 6,360 passengers and a crew of 2,100. Aside from a two-deck high dance hall, a 1380-seat theatre and an ice skating rink, a number of pools, spas, gyms, it also houses bars, restaurants and cafes as well as a shopping street with a park with trees.

> A water taxi is a small boat used for public transportation. Service maybe scheduled with multiple stops, operating in a similar manner to a bus or a taxi.

It names the Rising Tide Bar as one of its showpieces – an elliptical restaurant platform accommodating 50 customers that ascends and descends a vertical distance of 10 m between the central park and promenade.

WATER TRANSPORT

U.S.S. Constitution

The Constitution, called 'Old Ironsides' because cannonballs could not penetrate her tough oak sides, was one of the first of the original six frigates that made up the U.S. Navy. It is the oldest warship of the US Navy and the oldest commissioned warship afloat in the world. Still afloat after 213 years, she had an usually long service life, having remained in commission on and off between 1797 all the way to the Civil War, after which she was made a training ship and continued sailing periodically right up to her final decommissioning in 1881. During that time she fought in two conflicts: the First Barbary War—when she battled real pirates—and the War of 1812, during which she distinguished herself by defeating the British frigates HMS Guerriere and HMS Java. It was those engagements that gave her something of a reputation as a ship that could take on the British in a head-to-head fight, which was no small feat when one considers that the British Royal Navy was the largest and most powerful in the world at the time. Her fame saved her from the wrecking yard and in 1907 she began serving as a museum ship. Old Ironsides has been restored, refurbished and otherwise rebuilt so many times, it is said her keel is the only part of the original ship that remains, the rest having being replaced numerous times over the decades. She is also a still officially commissioned warship, with a sixty-man crew who are all active duty members of the United States Navy.

World's famous ships

MV Blue Marlin—World's largest transport ship

The MV Blue Marlin is a Dutch ship that was built in the year 2000 as a float-on/float-off or a heavy lift vessel that can be partially submerged. The Blue Marlin's cargo carrying capacity is around 30,000 tons and the ease with which the 154 m and 6,800 ton USS Cole was shipped from one part of the world to another, proves that the ship was designed to endure and carry cargo through.

The main reason the MV Blue Marlin was constructed was to provide a sort of base or anchorage to oil rigs. It has to be noted that the heavy lift vessel has several tiers which lower themselves into the water as and when required. This feature is the main USP of the Dutch naval vessel. Because of these tiers, the weight load of the cargo above is adequately balanced without any damage to it.

It has to be noted that all such heavy lift vessels including the Blue Marlin have cranes to lift and place the cargo on top of them. The total lift-off capacity of a crane at the very first lift is around 100 tons. This, once again proves the authenticity and reliability of a heavy lift vessel and more importantly, of the Blue Marlin in particular.

The main objective of heavy lift vessels such as the Blue Marlin is to provide cargo carrying facility to warships to ports and dry-docks for the purpose of repairing. It was only with the help of such a technology, that a very important naval warship was able to get restored back for a new naval life.

WATER TRANSPORT

Largest yacht— Eclipse

With a reported price tag of nearly $1.2 billion and a 170 m length, the Eclipse is not only the largest yacht, but also the most expensive. Russian billionaire Roman Abramovich's yacht Eclipse has received a huge amount of industry attention, not just for its size but for the celebrity of its owner.

> A submarine is a large vessel that operates below the water surface. The nickname of a submarine is sub, and the word submarine means under the water. It is a large, cylinder shaped 'boat' that is used for military, tourism or oil purposes.

The billionaire's mega yacht was constructed by the German ship construction company Blohm & Voss. It has two helicopter landing pads, its own mini submarine, 2 hot tubs and 2 regular pools and a cinema. The newest and most expensive yacht in the world also has anti rocket systems for preventing terrorist attacks and is fully bullet-proof. It also comes equipped with three launch boats, and a mini-submarine that is capable of submerging to 50 m. About 70 crew members are needed to operate the yacht.

As a new addition never before seen on mega yachts the Eclipse boosts a system that uses lasers to make it impossible for paparazzi to take photos. When activated the lasers automatically find all camera lenses pointing at the yacht and shine a laser on them thus making photographing impossible.

Yamato

Yamato, a Japanese battleship, is the world's largest battleship ever built, also mounting the largest calibre main armament ever built, at 18.1 inches in diameter. Yamato is named after the ancient Japanese Yamato Province, was a battleship of the Imperial Japanese Navy. She and her sister ship the Musashi were the largest, heaviest and most powerful battleships ever constructed, displacing 72,800 tons at full load, and armed with nine 46 cm (18.1 inch) main guns. The ship held special significance for the Empire of Japan as a symbol of the nation's naval power, and it's sinking by US aircraft in the final days of the war during the suicide **Operation Ten-Go** is sometimes considered symbolic of Japan's defeat itself.

Bismarck

Bismarck, a German battleship was one of the most famous warships of the 2nd World War. It was named after the 19th

century German chancellor Otto von Bismarck. It displaced more than 50,000 tons fully loaded and was the largest warship then commissioned. Her chief claim to fame came from the Battle of the Denmark Strait in May 1941 during which the battle cruiser HMS Hood, flagship of the Home Fleet and pride of the Royal Navy, was sunk within several minutes. In response, British Prime Minister Winston Churchill issued the order to 'Sink the Bismarck', spurring a relentless pursuit by the Royal Navy. Two days later, with safer waters almost in reach, Fleet Air Arm aircraft torpedoed Bismarck and jammed her rudder, allowing heavy British units to catch up with her. In the ensuing battle on the morning of May 27, 1941, Bismarck was heavily attacked for nearly three hours before sinking.

WATER TRANSPORT

Titanic

No other ship has captured the world's attention, quite like the Titanic. Constructed to be unsinkable, this first class ocean liner set sail on April 10, 1912. The world had awaited the maiden voyage of this luxury liner for months.

On the night of 14 April 1912, Titanic hit an iceberg, and sank two hours and forty minutes later, early on April 15, 1912. At the time of her launching in 1912, she was the largest passenger steamship in the world. The sinking resulted in the deaths of 1,517 people, one of the deadliest maritime disasters in history and by far the most famous. The discovery of the wreck in 1985 has made Titanic persistently famous in the years since.

Victoria

Victoria became famous in history because it was the first ship to successfully circumnavigate the world. The voyage was lead by Magellan and was accompanied by four other ships. Of this fleet of five, Victoria was the only ship to complete the voyage. Magellan himself was killed in the Philippines. The four other ships were Trinidad (110 tons, crew 55), San Antonio (120 tons, crew 60), Concepcion (90 tons, crew 45) and Santiago (75 tons, crew 32). Trinidad, Magellan's flagship, Concepcion, and Santiago were wrecked; San Antonio deserted the expedition before the Strait of Magellan and returned to Europe on her own. Victoria was rated a ship, as were all the others except Trinidad, which was a caravel.

A catamaran is a type of boat or ship consisting of two hulls joined by a frame. Catamarans can be sailed or engine-powered. The catamaran was the invention of the paravas, a fishing community in the southern coast of Tamil Nadu, India.

Test Your MEMORY

1. What do you mean by water transport?

2. Write briefly about the history of water transport.

3. Define the types of water transport.

4. Name the types of ships.

5. Name the important water transport routes.

6. What are seaports?

7. Write about the advantages of water transport.

8. Write about the disadvantages of water transport.

9. Write about water transport's importance to economy.

10. Write briefly about the Knock Nevis.

11. Name the largest bulk carrier ship in the world.

12. Name the largest yacht in the world.

WATER TRANSPORT

Index

A
Allure of the seas 25

B
Berge Stahl 23
Bismarck 29

C
cargo ship 6
container ships 10

D
deck covers 4
dry bulk ships 11
dugout boat 4

E
Eclipse 28
Emma Maersk 21

F
ferries 8

H
harbour 13
Hovercraft 5, 7

I
icebreakers 9
industrial ships 7

J
Jahre Viking 20

K
Knock Nevis 20

M
MV Blue Marlin 27

O
oars 4, 18
ocean liner 22, 30

P
paddlewheel boats 5

Q
Queen Mary 2 22

R
research vessels 9
rigging 4, 14
roll-on/roll-off ships (RORO) 11
rudders 4, 8, 24

S
sail 4, 5, 13, 22, 30
seaport 13, 14
steamship 5, 19, 30
stern 4, 8, 9, 10, 25

T
tankers 6
Titanic 10, 30

U
U.S.S. Constitution 26

V
Victoria 30

W
water transport 3, 4, 5, 12, 13, 15, 16, 17, 19

Y
Yamato 29